Ezekiel the Deaf Therapy Dog
Ezekiel Helps Clean the House

Luv hugs & kisses,
Ezekiel, Tom & Mary

Mary and Tom Lyons

ISBN 978-1-64003-552-2 (Paperback)
ISBN 978-1-64003-553-9 (Digital)

Copyright © 2018 Mary and Tom Lyons
All rights reserved
First Edition

All rights reserved. No part of this publication may be reproduced, distributed, or transmitted in any form or by any means, including photocopying, recording, or other electronic or mechanical methods without the prior written permission of the publisher. For permission requests, solicit the publisher via the address below.

Covenant Books, Inc.
11661 Hwy 707
Murrells Inlet, SC 29576
www.covenantbooks.com

INTRODUCTION

Ezekiel, the white boxer, was only three weeks old when we found out he was deaf. At five weeks old, the breeders were ready to find him a home. It was an extremely hard decision, but Tom and I decided to take Ezekiel into our home. It wasn't hard because he was deaf; it was hard because my husband was battling cancer at the time, and we didn't know how it was going to work out. The moment we brought Ezekiel into our home, he immediately gravitated to my husband, who had IVs twice a day administered by nurses. Ezekiel stayed in my husband's lap most of the day. We knew that there was something different about this goofy, deaf white boxer. We named him Ezekiel because it means "God strengthens." We loved him so much. He had a compassion and an empathy that we had never seen in a dog before. We started teaching Ezekiel ASL (American Sign Language) at six weeks old. He caught on extremely quickly. At six months, we enrolled him in two basic training classes. That was a struggle, but, somehow, we made it. Ezekiel couldn't concentrate or focus on my ASL signs, because all he was interested in was running after the lovely lady puppies. After he graduated, we started exposing Ezekiel to all kinds of situations. The whole purpose was getting him used to people, kids, and other dogs.

His disposition was remarkable. Right before his third birthday, we scheduled an interview with a Therapy Testing Organization. This was their first deaf dog to be tested, and they didn't know how it was going to work out, but that was okay. It didn't matter to us if he passed or failed. We loved Ezekiel no matter what. As we walked into the test site, I was so nervous; Ezekiel, on the other hand, was happy-go-lucky and ready to play. The state tester greeted us and started to give out directions. I interpreted to Ezekiel in ASL, and we ended up passing with a perfect score. We started going to nursing homes, youth groups at church, convalescent centers, independent living centers, and so many more. He comes to school with me on Fridays and ministers to the kids. I work at a school with special needs, and what a remarkable recovery some of the kids have made. Behaviors are slowly getting better. Ezekiel has been to a deaf school where the kids are able to sign to him. We just do it from the bottom of our hearts. We don't charge any fee. We don't ask for anything but some extra time to let our Ezekiel do his thing. Our next venture will be attending a juvenile prison and just helping some of the inmates feel better.

Ezekiel also has his certification in "Canines for Christ," where he can go to different churches and youth groups to minister the word. Our Ezekiel has impacted so many lives already. He makes someone smile for a minute, or even take away the emotional stress, or even take the physical pain away just for five minutes. That's what it's all about. Comforting those in need and just making a difference. This deaf little goofy puppy got my husband through so much. He brought my husband back to himself in ways no one can explain. I don't know where my husband would be today if it weren't for Ezekiel. I know in my heart Ezekiel made all the difference, and I am so grateful Tom is now cancer-free and in remission for three years. Ezekiel is really changing the hearts of so many, one person at a time.

Ezekiel now holds five certifications.

Therapy Dog

Canines for Christ

AKC Therapy Dog

AKC Therapy Dog Advanced

AKC Good Citizen

EZEKIEL HELPS CLEAN THE HOUSE

"Good morning, Ezekiel.
It's Saturday morning, and you know what that means
It's time for you to get up and help me clean the house."
"Okay, Mom, I'm coming," says Ezekiel.
See, I'm not a regular dog. I'm a goofy white boxer who was born deaf. But it's cool being deaf.
Mom taught me American Sign Language and
she is very patient.
I am a very special and unique puppy.
Okay, time to clean the bathroom.
Let's see . . . I need to wash the floor and just straighten up a bit.
Uh oh! My collar just got stuck on the toilet paper roll. Oh no!
I can't get it off.
Here comes, Mom.
"Ezekiel, what happened? My goodness, let me help you get that toilet paper off your collar."
Come on, let's go
we can work on cleaning the blinds.

There are so many blinds to clean
I don't remember what to do.
Mommy said
I'm not supposed
To use a ladder to clean them.
I think I got it.
If I pull them off, then I'll be able
To do a better job.
I did it. they are so clean.

Oh no! Now how do I get them back up?
Uh, oh!
Here comes Mom.
"Ezekiel, now what happened?
My goodness
Help me put these blinds back up.
Ezekiel, I think you need a two-minute
Time-out.
I'll meet you in the laundry room
We have to hang up some clothes."

This
Time-Out
Won't
Take too
Long.

Here I come, Mom.
My time-out is over.
Mom, I'm going to try and concentrate a little bit better.
Look, Mom dropped a hanger.
I'll just bring it to her.
Oh, wait, there's something wrong.
 Why is the top moving? I think it's broken.
I'll just fix it for her.
Uh oh…the top broke off and
 now the hanger
it's stuck on my face.
Mom . . . Mom . . . help me
"What is it now, Ezekiel? My goodness, how did
You get that stuck on your face?
Please be more careful, Ezekiel,
I don't want you to get hurt."

Whew!
It's been such a tiring morning.
Mom has me working hard today.
I think I'll just take a quick nap.
Oh, wait. What's this?
It's a box. It's a huge box.
I love boxes.
They are so much fun to rip up.
Maybe I should ask Mom
If I can rip up this box.
No, I think it's okay. It's by the front door,
Looks like it's ready for the trash.
"Ezekiel, Ezekiel,
Did you see the box that the comforter came in?
They sent the wrong size, and we have to return it today."
Uh oh! I think I'm in trouble again.

All right, I think I really am going to take a nap.
Let me grab this toy to sleep with.
Squeak, squeak, squeak.
This is my favorite squeaky toy. Where did it go?
Oh, I see it,
It went in the corner of the couch.
I got it. Uh oh, it's way down there.
Maybe if I just move this cushion.
I almost got it. I can almost reach it.
I got it.
Whew! That was hard.
What in the world is this fuzzy stuff
Around my waist?
Oh no!
The cushion broke.
I hope Mom is not too upset.
Mom! Mom! I need help again.
"Ezekiel."

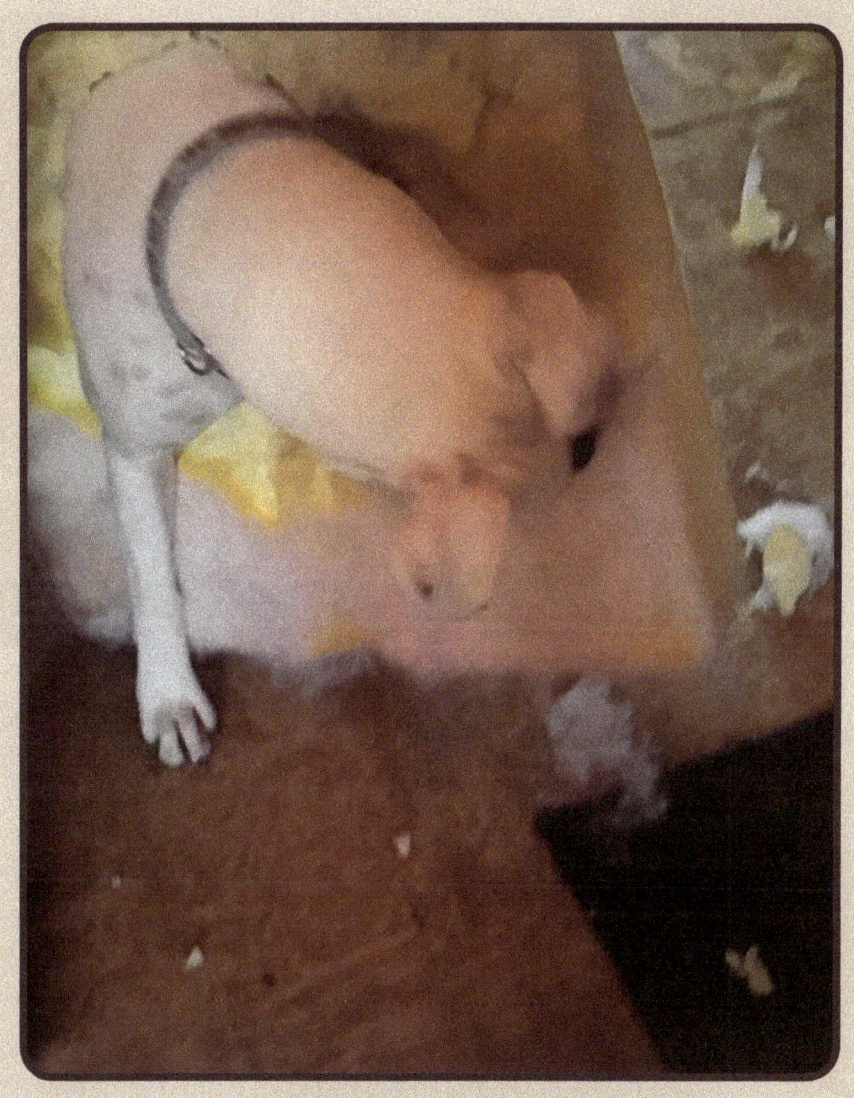

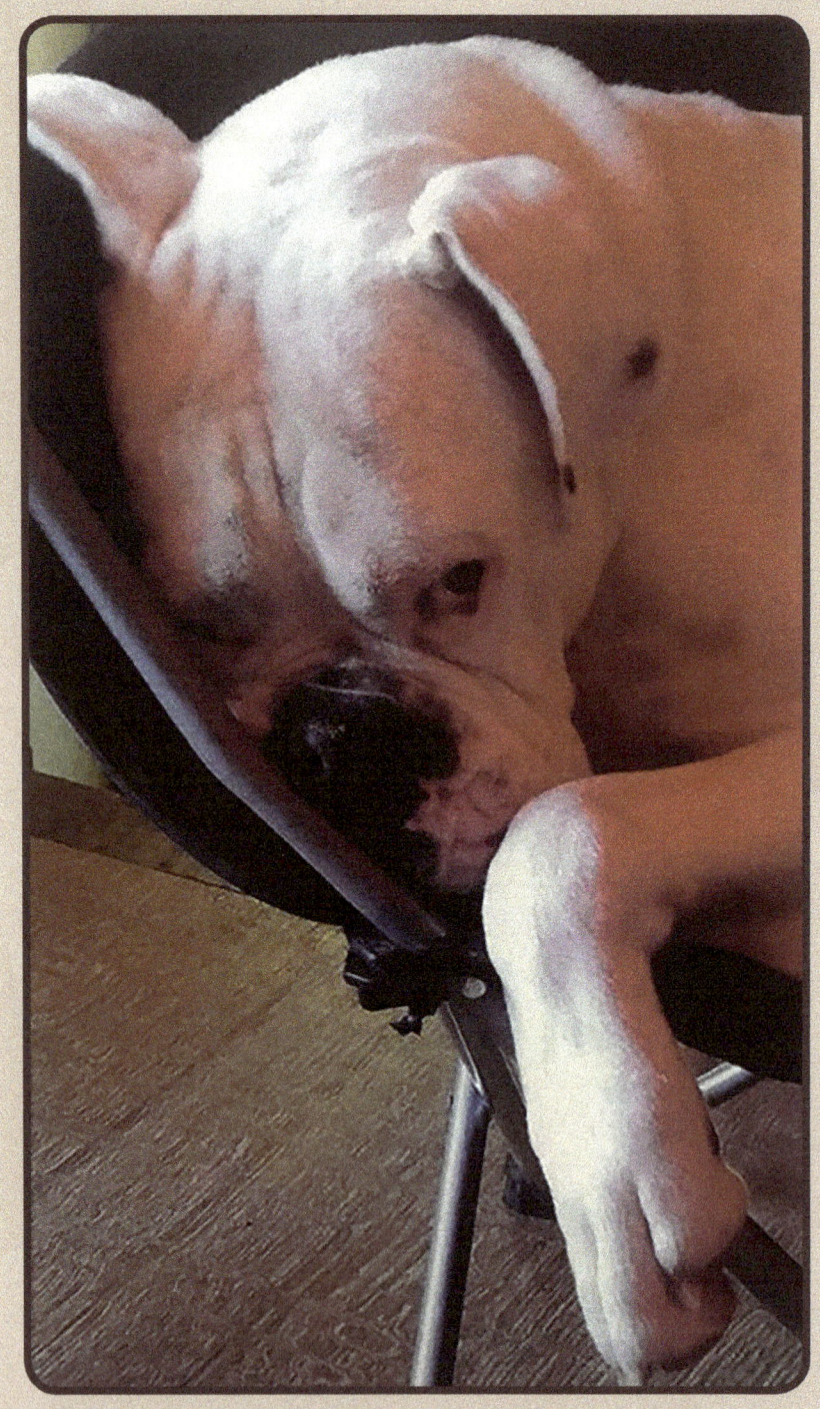

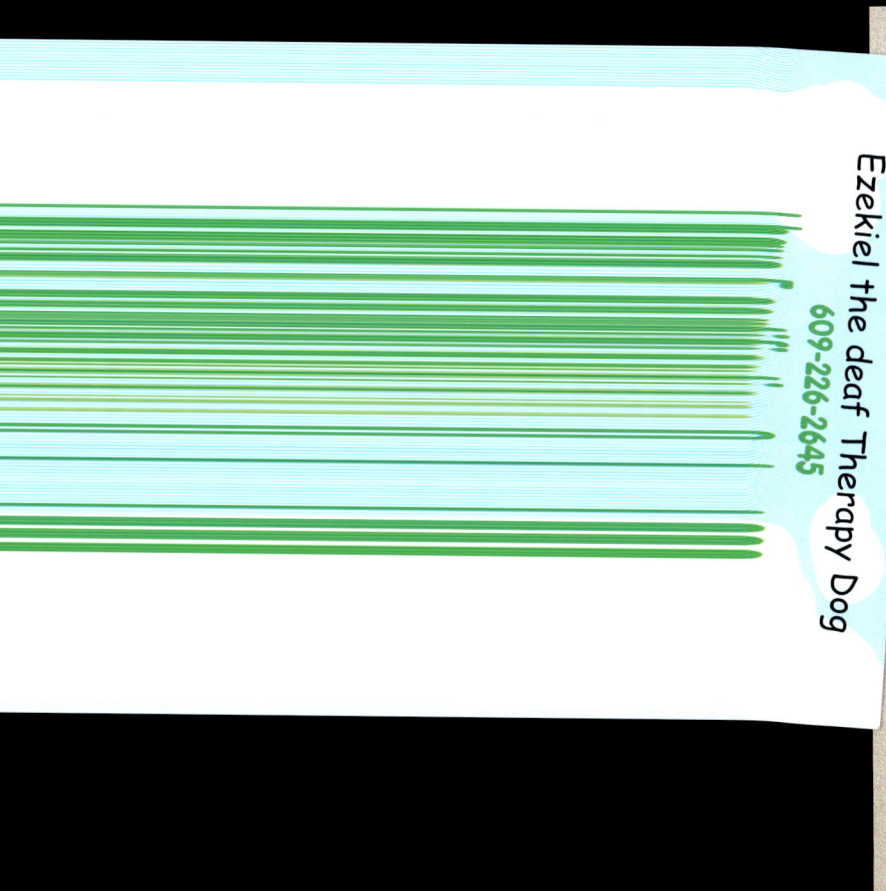

I'm
Sorry,
Mommy

I think I'm going to take a break
from this housework and
FaceTime my good buddy
Bowie,
who lives in Maine.
Hey, Bowie, how ya doing?
I'm having a fun day
Cleaning with my mommy.
Hope you are having a
Fun day.
Bowie, how was the Dog Park?
I know you love to run and play.
Mom and I were supposed
To go to the Dog Park,
but it's Saturday, and we must clean the house.
Maybe Mom will take me later.
Well, Bowie, I've got to go
Mom is calling me.

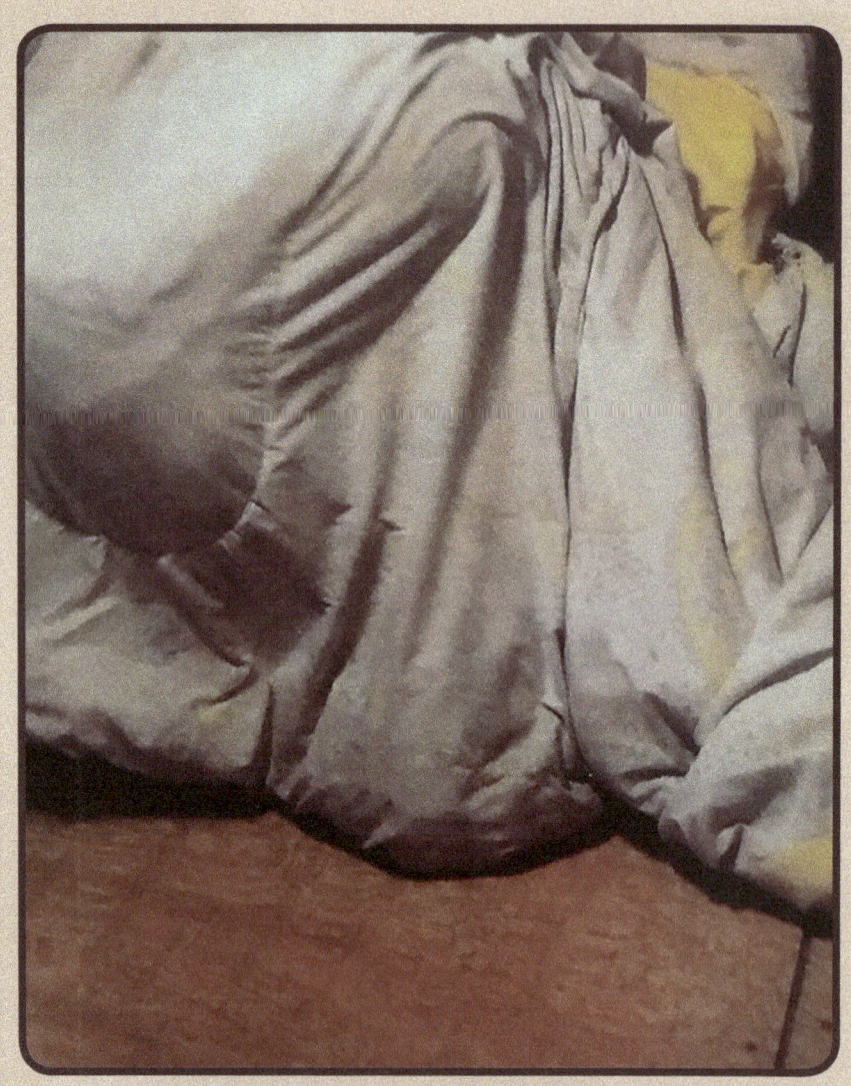

Here I am, Mom.
I hope we do not have a lot of cleaning left,
I'm kind of tired.
"Ezekiel, all we have left is to wash the comforters
and clean the curtains."
Okay that sounds very good. I'll get the
Comforter from Tommy's room
and bring it to you, Mommy.
This comforter is hard to drag, and it's too
Heavy to carry.
Oh no, I just slipped, the comforter is moving too fast. Wait, I can't see. Where did everyone go?
Mom! Mom! Mom!
Help me! I am stuck.
"Ezekiel, what happened? How did you get twisted up in this comforter? Hold on. Let me get you out.
"Ezekiel, please be still, you're almost untangled."
"Tell you what, Ezekiel, go pick up your toys. Then you can finish helping me a bit later."

All right, let me get the bucket
So I can clean up.
Wait, what happened?
The bucket won't move.
I think my foot is stuck.
Whew, I got it out. That was hard.
Okay, back to putting my toys away.
My goodness, look at
all these toys I left lying around.
I really did make a mess,
but I can't help it.
I love playing with balls, ropes,
squeaky toys, and stuffed animals.
Look, that didn't take too long
I'm almost finished.

Oh, look, I forgot to put this toy away.
Let me see if I can find my blue rope.
It's my favorite.
There it is in the bucket.
Let me find it,
It will only take a minute.
It's right there.
I can almost reach it.
Wait, let me dump this bucket
So I can grab it better,
Got it!

Wait a minute. What happened to the floor?
My toys got out again.
I really don't know how that
Happens all the time.
"Ezekiel, where are you?
I need you to help me take down the curtains."
Coming, Mom.

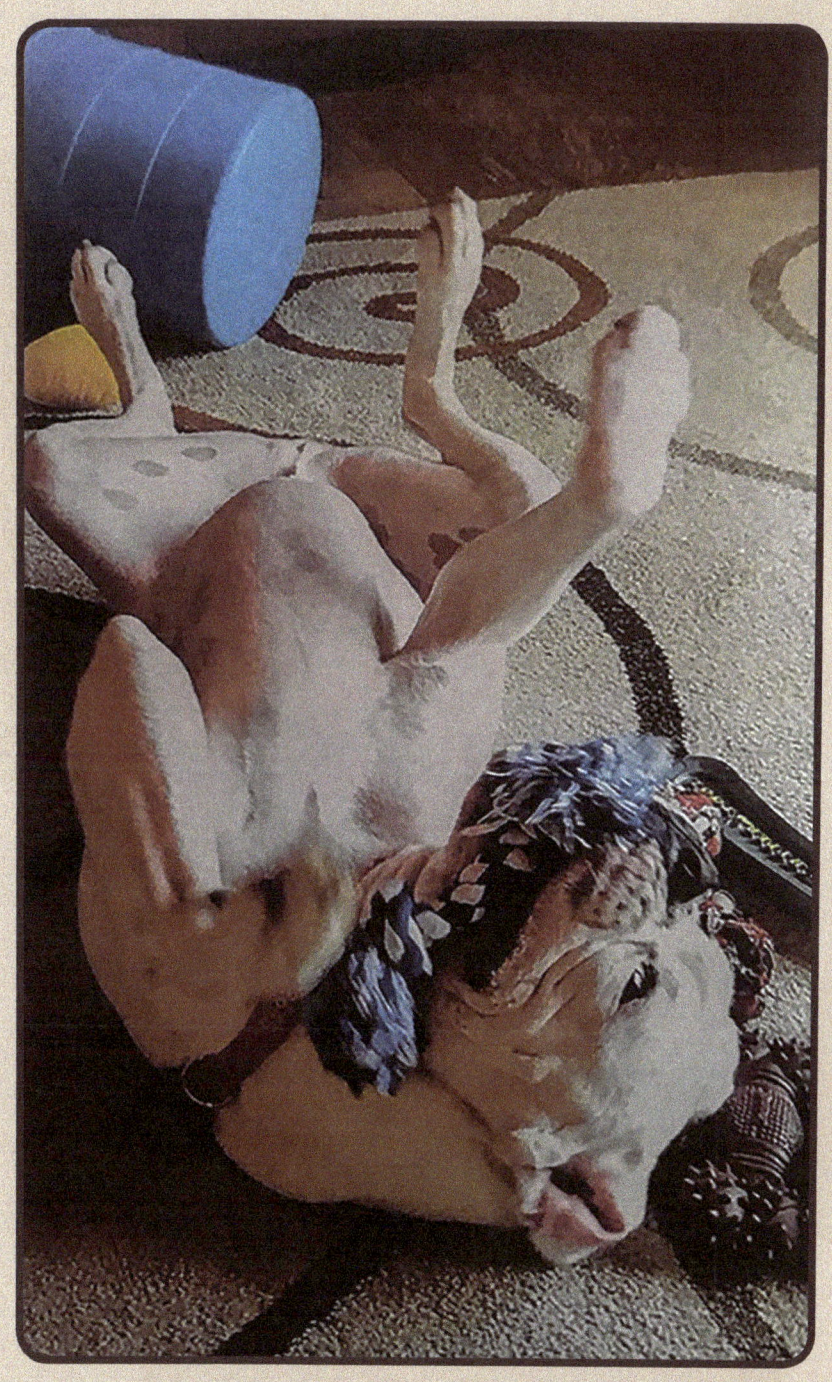

I am so tired from all this housecleaning.
I have not taken a nap all morning.
Cleaning the house is such hard work.
I'm glad we are almost done.
Oh, look, Mom, forgot these comforters
In the middle of the floor.
Maybe I will just take a short nap.
Zzzzzzz Zzzzzzz Zzzzzzz
"Ezekiel . . . Ezekiel . . .
Wake up!
If you're lying on the comforters how can
I finish the laundry."
Okay, Mom,
I'll meet you in the living room
And we can take down the curtains.

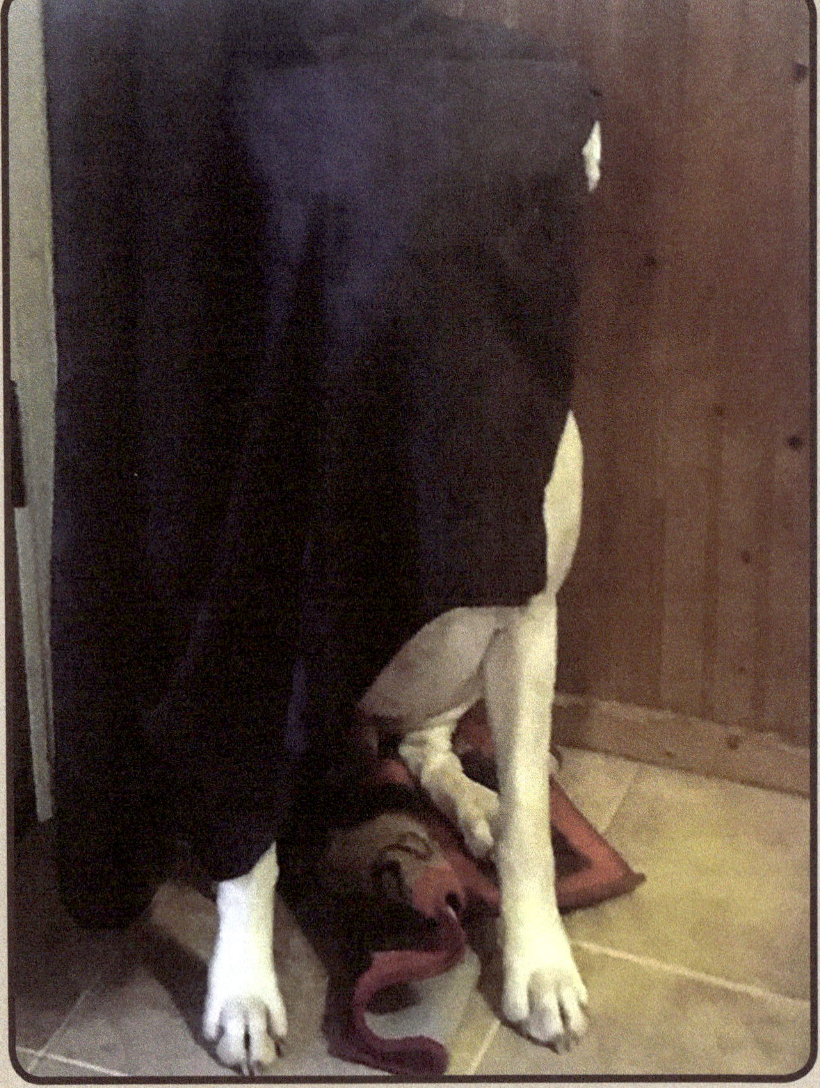

Where did she go?
Mom! Mom!
Ezekiel, I'm on the phone with Bowie's mom.
I'll be right there.
I love playing in the curtains.
Wait, I have an idea, maybe if I just
Hide, Mom won't see me.
Here she comes.
"Ezekiel, Ezekiel where are you?
Oh, my, you are such a silly boy.
Please get out from those curtains
So I can finish my cleaning.
I'll tell you what
Why don't you go outside
and play for a while?
Maybe you can help Daddy with the yard work.
Wow, Mom, that sounds like a lot of fun.
"See you later, Ezekiel."

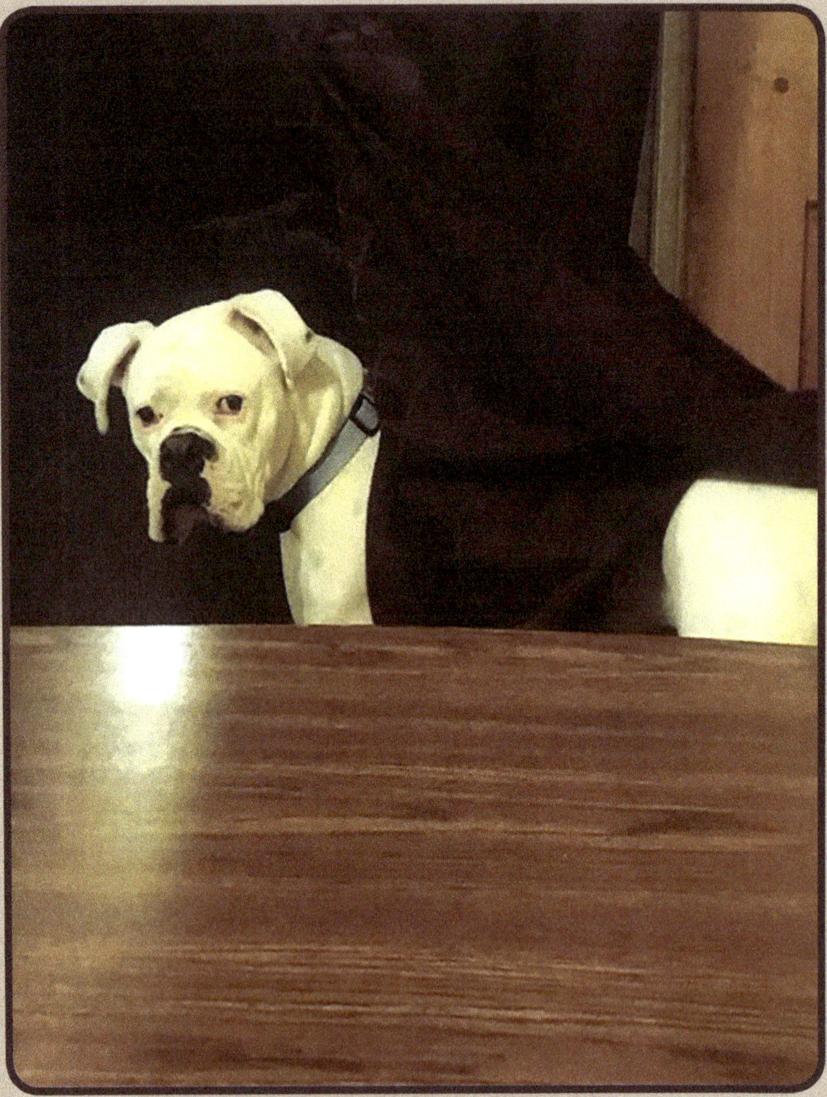

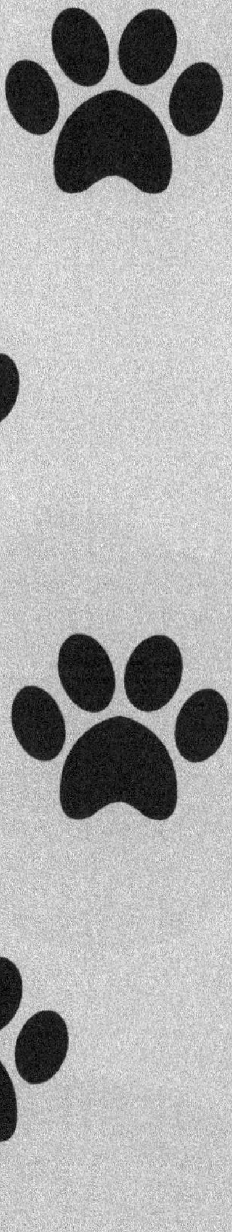

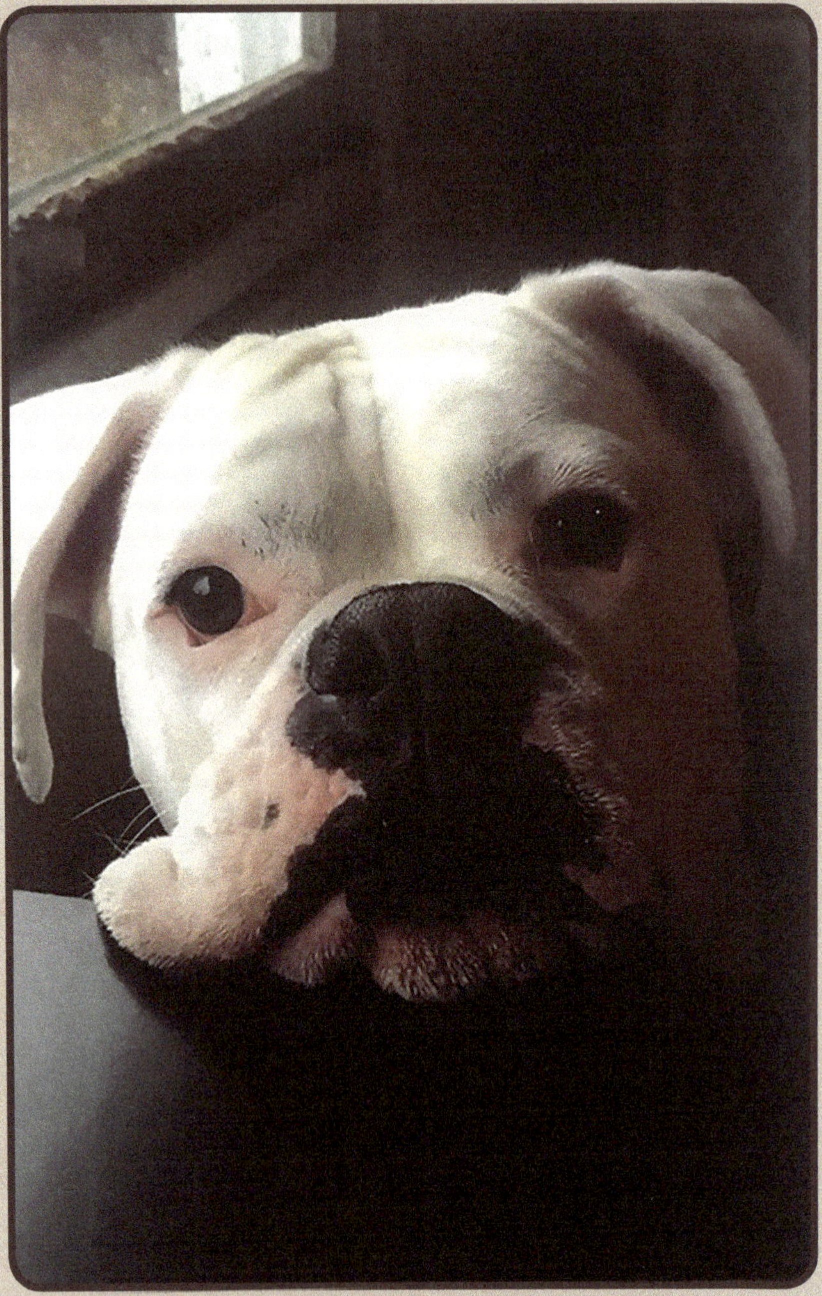

Bye-bye
See
You soon
Love,
Ezekiel

ABOUT THE AUTHORS

Tom and Mary Lyons have resided in Tuckahoe, New Jersey, for the past twenty-one years. Mary is a special education science teacher and plans on retiring next year. She is also part of the local Rescue Squad as a chaplain in training. Tom is a residential electrician who has been in the trade for thirty years. He also enjoys cooking and barbecuing gourmet meals. One of their favorite pastimes has been fostering special need dogs over the past twenty years. They are also very active in their church, doing various ministries.

To find out more about Ezekiel and his family, check out his Facebook page at
Ezekiel the deaf Therapy Dog.

CPSIA information can be obtained
at www.ICGtesting.com
Printed in the USA
BVHW09s2233200918
528001BV00014B/148/P